GREAT ILLUSTRATED CLASSICS

GULLIVER'S TRAVELS

Jonathan Swift

adapted by
Malvina G. Vogel

Illustrations by
Pablo Marcos

**BARONET
BOOKS**

BARONET BOOKS, New York, New York

Contents

About the Author

Abigaile Swift was only 20 and in debt when her 21-year-old husband died, leaving her with a one-year-old daughter and expecting another child. That other child, born on November 30, 1667 in Dublin, Ireland, was Jonathan Swift.

While Jonathan was still very young, Mrs. Swift took her daughter and returned to England, leaving her son to be raised in Dublin by relatives who could send him to a fine school and to Trinity College to study for the priesthood in the Church of Ireland.

However, after graduation, 21-year-old Jonathan preferred to take a job in England as secretary to Sir William Temple, a writer and diplomat. At Temple's estate, Jonathan read extensively in the vast library. He met writers, scholars, and wealthy politicians of the day. And he began developing the talent he would one day be famous for—writing satire, witty articles that ridiculed famous people, foolish ideas, and absurd customs.

In London, Swift made friends with other satirists of the day and together, they formed the Martinus Scriblerus Club. One project was the joint writing of a satire ridiculing the arts, sciences, and politics of modern men. Each club member was given a subject to write his satire on. Swift's was travel books about far-away lands, for these had become very popular and fashionable in London society.

Working on this project inspired Swift, and it wasn't very long afterwards that the book's hero, Martin Scriblerus, turned into Lemuel Gulliver and the faraway lands became Lilliput and Brobdingnag. When *Gulliver's Travels* was published in 1726, the book was such an immediate success that its first printing sold out in a week! It is considered a masterpiece of satire today, over 260 years later, and is still read by adults for its irony and wit, and by children because it's such a delightfully funny adventure tale.

Jonathan Swift died in 1745 at the age of seventy-eight, but he is still considered the greatest satirist in the history of English literature.

Doctor Lemuel Gulliver

Chapter 1

Shipwrecked!

I'm not an old man writing down my life story, for I expect that many years and many adventures lay ahead of me yet, for I'm only forty-two years old. Still, during those years, I've had many strange adventures in my travels to far-off lands of the world.

Perhaps strange adventures aren't what you'd expect from someone named *Doctor* Lemuel Gulliver, but being a doctor in London or anyplace in England or anyplace on land, for that matter, just didn't satisfy me. Even when I was a medical student, I made certain to take courses in navigation, for travel to distant places in the world always fascinated me.

After graduating from medical school at the age of twenty-four, I signed up as a ship's doctor and spent three and a half years sailing around Europe and throughout the Mediterranean Sea.

On my return to England, I married and set up a practice in London. But at the end of two years, I realized that I couldn't make a success of medicine on land, and with my wife's approval I went to sea again.

For the next six years, I traveled to the East and West Indies as a ship's doctor, earning money to send home to my family and learning many languages during my time ashore in foreign lands. Because I have an excellent memory, I learned these languages very easily—a talent which would prove to be very useful during the voyages I would make afterwards.

At the end of those six years, I had grown

"Travel Fascinated Me."

tired of the sea and tried again to practice medicine on land, this time in a coastal village, where I could treat sailors. But this practice was no more successful than my earlier one. So, after three years on land, I accepted an offer from William Prichard, captain of the *Antelope*, to become the ship's doctor on a voyage to the South Seas.

We set sail from Bristol, England, on May 4, 1699, and after peacefully crossing the South Seas, we hit a violent storm off the west coast of Australia. Poor food and overwork while braving the storm caused the death of twelve of our crew and weakened the rest. So when the wind drove us onto some rocks and split the ship apart, only six seamen, myself included, had enough strength to get a lifeboat down into the sea and row clear of the ship and rocks.

Even though we were all exhausted, we kept rowing until we couldn't lift our arms any longer. After that, we lay back and let the

A Violent Storm

waves carry us wherever they wished.

A strong blast of wind from the north suddenly overturned our little boat and scattered my five companions. I never again laid eyes on them or on those I had last seen on the *Antelope*. I can only assume that they were all lost at sea.

As for me, I began to swim in whichever direction the wind and the waves were pushing me. I don't know how many hours I spent struggling against the waves, but just when I felt my last drop of strength leaving me and water was beginning to fill my lungs, my feet suddenly touched bottom.

I took in several mouthfuls of air and looked up to heaven. From the color of the sky, I guessed it was about eight o'clock in the evening. The storm had decreased, and there was enough light left to make out land about a mile away. I spent the next two hours dragging myself towards the shore.

The Boat Overturned.

Tied to Pegs Fastened into the Ground

Chapter 2

A Prisoner in Lilliput

I was so weak and tired when I finally limped out of the sea that I dropped down on a patch of soft grass. Within moments, I was sound asleep.

I must have slept for about nine hours, for when I awoke, it was daylight. I tried to get up, but found I couldn't move. My arms and legs were tied to pegs fastened into the ground. Thin, strong cords were tied across my body from my armpits to my thighs, and these were also attached to pegs in the ground. My long hair was spread out and tied down in the same manner.

All I could do was stare upwards at the sun, blinking to ease the pain on my already strained eyes. Suddenly, I heard strange noises around me, but I couldn't move to find out what they were or where they were coming from.

The next moment, I felt something alive moving on my left leg. It progressed over my stomach and onto my chest, stopping just below my chin. I lowered my eyes downward as much as I could, hoping to see what sort of insect was crawling on me. Then I suddenly gasped, "Why, it's a human creature barely six inches tall!"

This creature had a bow and arrow in his hands, and was followed by about forty more of these same creatures. I was so astonished that I let out a frightful roar. This sent all the tiny creatures running backwards and jumping off my body in terror.

However, they soon returned, and one of

Barely Six Inches Tall

them even climbed onto my chin to get a closer look at my face. Upon seeing it, he let out a screeching cry of astonishment. *"Hekinah degul!"*

"Hekinah degul!" repeated the others.

I had no idea what those words meant and didn't pay too much attention to them. My only thought was to get loose, for I was becoming quite uncomfortable. By twisting and turning, and pulling and pushing, I managed to break the strings and pull out the pegs that were holding my left arm down. With that arm released, I was able to free my hair on the left side and turn my head to the right.

I then tried to reach out and grab some of the creatures, but they ran off again, this time with shrieks of *"Tolgo phonac!"*

The next instant, hundreds of tiny arrows hit my left hand, pricking me like hundreds of needles. More hit my body, but my clothes kept them from sticking into me. But when arrows began striking my face, I groaned with pain

Hundreds of Tiny Arrows

and raised my left hand to try to protect myself.

I tried again to loosen the rest of my strings, only to be attacked with even more arrows than before. These little creatures also began jabbing spears at my sides, but lucky for me, my leather vest kept those spears from entering my body.

I then told myself, "The wisest thing to do, Lemuel, is to lie still until night. Then, you'll be able to use your left hand to free the rest of your body, and even the greatest armies of these tiny people won't be able to stand up to someone your size!"

So, I stopped struggling and the arrows stopped coming. But I soon heard another noise near my right ear. It was a banging, like people at work. I turned my head as much as I could and saw about fifty of these little people setting up a platform a foot and a half above the ground.

Soon, four of the little people climbed up lad-

They Were Jabbing Spears at My Sides.

ders and stood on the platform. In the middle was an important-looking man with an attendant on each side and a page behind him, carrying the train of his robe. The man made a long speech in my direction, and of course, I didn't understand one single word of it. But I could tell from the tone of his voice that some words were threats, others were promises, and still others were reassurances, especially when he pointed all around him and repeated over and over, *"Lilliput! Lilliput!"*

So, I was in a place called Lilliput, though I had never heard of such a country or seen it on a map. I tried to answer this important man, using a few words of English, to explain that I was a friend and meant them no harm. I even raised my eyes and hand to heaven to make my promise even stronger.

The last time I had eaten was hours before the ship sank, so I had to show these people that I was desperate for food. I did it by putting my fingers into my mouth as I spoke.

"Lilliput! Lilliput!"

The great *Hurgo*, as I later learned this important lord was called, understood my signs and shouted out orders to the crowd below. A hundred little people immediately placed ladders at my sides and climbed up on my body with baskets full of meat and bread, which they dumped into my mouth. This was food their Emperor had ordered as soon as he received word of my arrival.

When I signaled that I was also thirsty, they rolled a barrel up a ladder and across my chest. Then they poured into my mouth a delicious liquid that tasted like wine. But their barrel was only equal to a cup, and after they had given me a second barrel, they showed me that they had no more.

By now, I was feeling very grateful to these little people. They treated me generously and were brave enough to walk on my body even though my free hand was capable of crushing any one of them if I wished.

Once I had finished eating, a high-ranking

Climbing Up My Body with Baskets of Food

minister from the Emperor climbed onto my leg followed by twelve attendants. The minister approached my face and spoke, pointing often to something in the distance and calling it *Mildendo*. The minister was trying to explain that the Emperor wanted me taken to Mildendo, Lilliput's capital city.

With my free left hand, I tried to signal to him that I would like to be untied. The minister understood, but shook his head no and made a sign that I was to be carried to Mildendo as a prisoner. But he also made a sign that I would be fed and treated well.

I still had blisters and sores on my face to remind me what their arrows could do and since there were now many more of these little people around me, I nodded to show that I would not give them any trouble.

Seeing that his mission was a success, the minister climbed down from my body. Soon, dozens of little people were crawling over my face and hands, dabbing at them with a sweet-

I Tried to Signal.

smelling ointment that took away the sting of the arrows.

With my body now a little more comfortable, I soon became drowsy and fell into another deep sleep, this time for eight hours. I later learned that the Emperor had ordered his physician to mix some sleeping powder into my wine so he could make plans to have me brought to the capital.

It seems that when I was discovered on the shore, the Emperor immediately ordered five hundred engineers and carpenters to build the largest flat car ever made in the kingdom. They already had many huge vehicles on wheels for hauling tall trees, but this one was a wood frame seven feet long and four feet wide. It was raised three inches off the ground and set on twenty-two wheels.

The flat car had been pulled alongside me as I slept, but was already underneath me when I woke up.

"How could these little people have lifted me

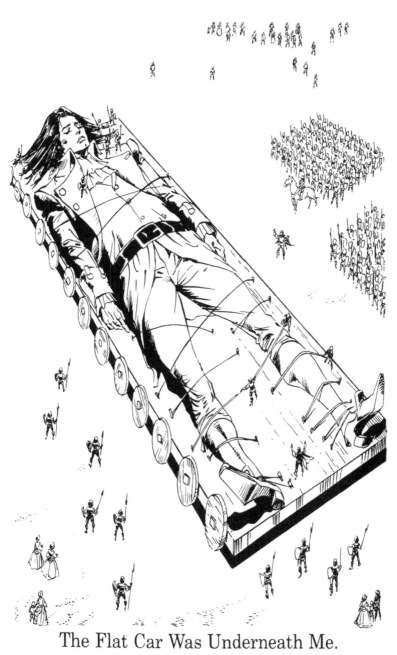

The Flat Car Was Underneath Me.

and placed me on this vehicle?" I asked myself in amazement.

I later learned that brilliant Lilliputian minds had devised a system of pulleys to raise me and place me on the flat car. It took nine hundred of their strongest men pulling on the cords around my body to do it, but they did it in three hours as I lay in a drugged sleep.

They also had fifteen hundred of the Emperor's largest horses, each about four and half inches high, harnessed to the vehicle to pull me. With five hundred guards on each side of me, we began the half-mile trip to Mildendo. We traveled all day through the colorful countryside, passing clusters of trees reaching seven feet into the sky. After resting at night, we arrived at the gates to the city about noon.

The Emperor came out to meet us, but his advisors wouldn't permit him to expose himself to danger by climbing onto my body. Instead, he and his lords climbed up onto a five-foot-high turret on the city wall. From here,

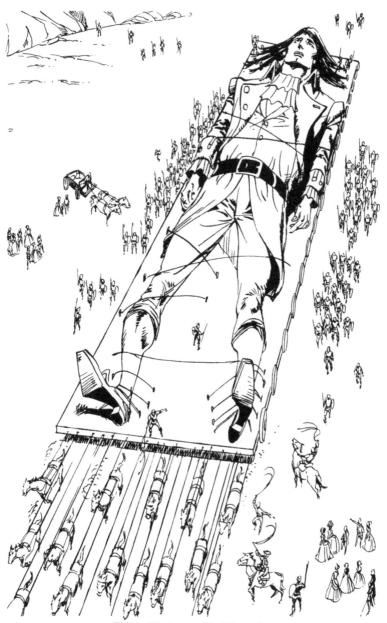

The Trip to Milendo

they could study me. Down on the ground, more than 100,000 curious Lilliputians were studying me as well.

As the Emperor began speaking, he motioned to a huge, deserted building about twenty feet away. It was an ancient temple that was now abandoned because a murder had been committed there. This was the only building in Lilliput large enough for me to crawl into and live in, since it was four feet high and had a gate two feet wide.

Royal blacksmiths had already fastened a hundred chains to the wall near the gate. When I arrived, these chains were fastened to my left leg with thirty-six padlocks.

When the Emperor was assured that I couldn't break loose from the chains, he ordered the workmen to cut the cords with which I had been tied during the trip here.

I immediately stood up and stretched my stiff body. Then I walked back and forth outside the temple, even though it was only for

The Emperor Began Speaking.

two yards—the length of my chains. Seeing my size and movement brought cries of astonishment from the Lilliputians.

Now that I was standing, I could look out and see what Lilliput looked like. Mildendo, the capital city, was built in a perfect square. Surrounding it was a two-foot-high wall, five hundred feet long on each side. Its twelve-inch thickness made it wide enough for coaches and horses to travel on.

Inside the wall, the city had two five-foot-wide main streets which crossed each other in the center at the royal palace. Narrow lanes and alleys barely a foot wide led off the main streets. Houses three, four and five stories high filled the city, and hundreds of well-stocked shops and markets served the city's 500,000 inhabitants.

This tiny town was to be my new home!

The Lilliputians' Capital

The Emperor Approached Me.

Chapter 3

The Search For Weapons

When I finished my stretching and walking, I crawled into the temple to explore the inside of my new "house." I was pleased to discover that there was enough room for me to stretch out on the floor to have some privacy when I slept.

When I came back out, the Emperor climbed down from the turret and approached me on horseback. He showed no fear, but his horse reared up at the sight of something that looked like a mountain to him—me! The Emperor, however, was an excellent horseman and kept his balance in the saddle while he calmed his steed, then dismounted.

Even though His Majesty stayed beyond my reach, he gazed up at me with great admiration. I decided to lie down to get a better look at this tiny creature, who stood just under seven inches tall. I saw a proud, strong man of about thirty years old. His robes were simple, but his gold helmet, with a crest of jewels, left no doubt of his royal position. He held his three-inch-long, diamond-covered sword in his hand in case I broke my chains as he came closer.

The Emperor began to speak and I answered him, although neither of us understand one word the other was saying. He ordered his advisors—I judged them to be priests and lawyers from their clothing—to speak to me as well. I answered in as many languages as I knew—English, Dutch, Latin, French, Spanish, Italian—but it was no use. None came even close to Lilliputian. I determined I would learn quickly to use their language.

To Get a Better Look

The Emperor signaled to his cooks and butlers standing behind him. Twenty carts of meat were pushed towards me, giving me three good mouthfuls. Ten carts held clay jugs of wine. I emptied all the jugs into one cart and came up with one mouthful!

Once the Emperor saw that I was properly fed, he turned to go. But he left a large number of guards to protect me from the curious crowd eager to swarm all over me and from the malicious troublemakers who shot their arrows into me when they thought no one was looking.

When one arrow nearly hit my eye, the colonel of the guards ordered six of the troublemakers seized and tied up. Then he pushed them at spear point towards my right hand for me to punish them. I scooped up all six and put five into my pocket. Then I lifted the sixth up to my face, opening my mouth as if I planned to eat him alive.

The poor man screamed, and the frightened

Carts of Meat, Jugs of Wine

crowd gasped as I took my knife from my pocket and brought it up to the terrified man's throat. Then I innocently began cutting the ropes from his wrist and gently placed him on the ground. I did the same with the other five, and all six ran from me and scattered in the crowd as quickly as they could. I noticed that all the Lilliputians were very impressed at the mercy I had shown to their people.

After I spent the first few nights sleeping on the stone floor of my house, the Emperor gave orders for a bed to be prepared for me. Workers brought in six hundred mattresses and laid them down in four layers of one hundred fifty mattresses each. They also prepared sheets and blankets for me.

Curious Lilliputians came from all over the kingdom to see me, even neglecting their work, their lands, and their families. The Emperor finally had to order them back to their homes and decree that anyone wishing to see me had to get permission from the Secretary

All Six Ran From Me.

of State and pay a fee for it.

Meanwhile, the Emperor was meeting with his advisors to decide what should be done with me. One particular Lilliputian who had become my friend informed me what was happening.

"There are some at Court who fear you'll get loose," he told me. "Others fear that feeding you will cause starvation among our people. There are even some who want to shoot poison arrows into you and kill you, but fear that your huge body could cause a plague once it begins to decay."

"And what did they decide?" I asked.

"In the middle of all these discussions, several officers entered the council chamber and told of your merciful act in sparing the lives of the six Lilliputians who had been shooting arrows into you. The Emperor was so impressed with your actions that he issued a decree requiring the surrounding villages to deliver to the palace each morning six oxen, forty sheep,

The Emperor Was Meeting with His Advisors.

bread, and wine for you. He'll pay the villagers for all this from his own personal gold, for he never forces his subjects to support him or his family."

"That's unheard of in my country!" I said.

"His Majesty has also hired six hundred servants to wait on you, and he even built tents for them to live in at your door. Among these servants are the royal tailors, who will make a suit of clothes for you."

The Emperor's concern for me didn't stop there. He sent six of his greatest scholars to teach me and even helped in my lessons himself. I had learned the Lilliputian language quite well in about three weeks, and my first words to the Emperor were: "Please, Your Majesty, set me free!"

His answer came with a sigh. "Be patient, my new friend. We are treating you kindly. When the time comes, you'll be set free."

Then he surprised me by his next request. "Would you be offended if I asked you to agree

My First Words to the Emperor

to be searched? It is a law in Lilliput. A person of your great size could be hiding dangerous weapons. Of course, anything we take from you will be returned when you leave our country."

"Your Majesty, I'd be willing to turn my pockets inside out or even take off all my clothes to assure you I have no weapons and no evil intentions." I said this partly in words and partly by signs.

I then picked up the officers the Emperor chose and put them first in my jacket pockets, then my trouser pockets. But I kept the one with my glasses, compass, and telescope hidden. I didn't want to risk losing them.

The officers made a list of everything they found, and when they were finished, they showed it to me. Their writing was very peculiar; it wasn't done from left to right like English, or right to left like Arabian, or top to bottom like Chinese. Lilliputian writing was done on a slant from one corner of the paper to the

I Put the Officers in My Pockets.

opposite one.

I read the list before they presented it to the Emperor. "In the right jacket pocket of the Great Man-Mountain (for that is what they named me), we found one huge piece of coarse cloth large enough to be a rug in Your Majesty's throne room (my handkerchief) and a thick board covering a folded bundle of thin, white paper filled with black marks and tied with a strong cord (my journal).

"In the left pocket was a huge silver chest which was too heavy for us to lift out. When the Man-Mountain opened it for us, we stepped into it and found ourselves up to our knees in some white dust that made us sneeze (my snuff box). Also in this pocket was some sort of machine with twenty long poles sticking out all in a row (my comb).

"In the right pocket of his trousers was a hollow iron tube about as long as two men. It was attached to a strong piece of wood. The iron was cut out with an opening for the Man-

I Read the List.

Mountain's finger to slip in and make a clicking noise. We don't know what sort of strange machine this is (my pistol).

"In the left pocket were two flat iron sticks as tall as we were. A shiny steel plate seemed to be hidden in each stick and we asked the Man-Mountain to show us what these were since they seemed like dangerous weapons. He showed us that they opened up, one to shave his beard and the other to cut his meat.

"Two pockets formed slits in his vest. Out of the right one hung a silver chain with a wonderful round engine at the bottom. Half of it was silver and the other half, some transparent metal covering strange figures drawn in a circle. A pointed arrow moved slowly around the circle and made a continuous sound, as if it were alive. We think it is either some unknown animal or a god he worships, since he told us he always consults it when he does anything (my watch).

"From the other slit pocket he drew out a net

A Wonderful Round Engine

that opened like a purse. Inside were several huge pieces of yellow metal which, if they are gold, would have great value.

"Around his middle, the Man-Mountain wears a belt made of the skin of some animal. From this belt hangs a sword as long as five of our men and a pouch with two compartments. One contained several metal balls the size of our head (bullets) and the other, a pile of light-weight black grains (gunpowder).

"This is the exact list of what we found on the Man-Mountain's body. Signed and sealed this 4th day of the 89th moon of Your Majesty's most magnificent reign.

"Signed: Clefen Frelock, Marsi Frelock."

I handed the list to the Emperor, who read it and asked to see my sword. I pulled it out of its sheath, and the dazzling glare of the sun shining on its steel surface stunned and terri-fied the troops.

"Please place this weapon on the ground," said the Emperor. And I did.

The Emperor Asked to See My Sword.

"Please take out the strange hollow iron tube that your finger fits into and show me how it works."

I took out my pistol and showed him how I loaded it. Before I pulled the trigger, I warned him, "It will make a very loud noise, but don't be afraid. No one will get hurt."

Still, the noise astonished the crowd so much that many of them fell to the ground as if they had actually been hit.

As I placed the pistol and pouch on the ground, I begged the Emperor, "Please keep the pouch away from any fire. It can explode from the smallest spark and destroy the entire city."

"Your possessions will be treated with care, just as you will be, Man-Mountain," the Emperor assured me. "You have my word on it."

Many of Them Fell to the Ground.

Children Played Hide and Seek in My Hair.

Chapter 4

Unlocking The Chains

My gentleness with the people and my good behavior seemed to impress the Emperor and his advisors, as well as the Lilliputians themselves. As they lost their fear of me, they enjoyed dancing on my hand and even let their children play hide and seek in my hair. I encouraged these friendships in the hope that the people would persuade the Emperor to remove my chains.

His Majesty often had shows put on outside my house. I was especially impressed by the skill and grace of the rope-dancers, who performed on a thin white thread two feet above the ground. But I was shocked to learn that these performances were competitions to select important ministers at Court. Whoever was the best dancer and jumped the highest on the rope would be named a minister. Even those who were already in office were often required to dance on the rope to prove that they hadn't lost their skills.

Flimnap, the Court Treasurer, got his job by jumping one inch higher than any other lord in the kingdom and doing several somersaults on a wooden board balanced on the rope. Reldresal, the Emperor's Private Secretary who became my good friend, is almost as good as Flimnap.

In another competition, the Emperor holds a stick straight out in front of him, changing its height every few minutes. The competitors have to leap over the stick or creep under it at each turn. The winner is the one who does the most graceful leaping and creeping, and who

The Best Jumper Would Be Minister.

stays in the competition the longest. Blue, red, and green silk ribbons are awarded to the first, second, and third place winners, who proudly wear their awards tied around their waist.

As the horses began to lose their fear of me, their riders were able to exercise them by having them leap over my hand as I held it on the ground. One huntsman even made an amazing leap over my foot, shoe and all!

As the weeks went by, I continued begging the Emperor to set me free. Every minister in his Council urged him to do so, except Skyresh Bolgolam, the High Admiral of the Realm, who for some unknown reason had chosen to be my enemy. He was finally persuaded by the others to go along with their decision, but he insisted that first I had to swear to a list of conditions that he would draw up.

When the list was ready, the High Admiral himself came to me to read them. *"Golbasto Momaren Evlame Gurdilo Shefin Mully Ully*

The Horses Leap Over My Hand.

Gue, the most mighty Emperor of Lilliput," he began, "the Delight and Terror of the Universe whose feet press down to the center of the earth and whose head reaches up to the sun, proposes that the Man-Mountain must agree to the following conditions:

"That the Man-Mountain will not leave our kingdom without the Emperor's permission;

"That he will not come into our capital city without our permission and by giving two hours warning so people can stay in their houses;

"That he shall walk only on our main roads and not lie down in our fields;

"That as he walks he is careful not to step on our people, their horses or their carriages;

"That he not pick up any of our people without their consent;

"That he shall be willing to carry the Emperor's messengers and horses on important journeys to distant lands and return them safely;

"The Man-Mountain Must Agree."

"That he shall help Lilliput in the war against its enemies on the island of Blefuscu and destroy the Blefuscudian fleet, which is now preparing to invade Lilliput;

"That he shall help our workmen lift heavy stones as they build walls;

"That he shall measure the circumference of Lilliput by walking around the entire coast.

"If the Man-Mountain agrees to all this, he shall have a daily allowance of meat and drink equal to that of 1,728 of our people. So ordered by His Majesty on this twelfth day of the 91st moon of his reign."

"I agree to the Emperor's conditions," I replied, though I secretly knew that some of the conditions were the evil doings of Skyresh Bolgolam himself.

"Then you must swear to these conditions according to the laws of Lilliput."

"I agree. What do the laws of Lilliput require me to do?"

"You must hold your right foot in your left

"What Do the Laws Require?"

hand, place the middle finger of your right hand on top of your head and your thumb on the tip of your right ear, and whisper the Emperor's name as you do it."

By now, nothing surprised me about this land and its people, so I agreed to this as well.

"Golbasto Momaren Evlame Gurdilo Shefin Mully Ully Gue, the most mighty Emperor of Lilliput," I whispered as I twisted my arms and legs into the foolish position the High Admiral requested.

Then, once I had untwisted myself, Skyresh Bolgolam unlocked my chains. I was free at last!

Free At Last!

I Climbed Over the City Wall.

Chapter 5

The Threat Of War

My first request was to see the inside of Mildendo. The Emperor gave me permission, but cautioned me to be careful of the people and their homes. The people were told in advance of my visit, and everyone hurried indoors, not only to protect themselves but to watch me from their top-floor windows.

Leaving my long jacket at home so it wouldn't strike someone's roof, I gently and carefully climbed over the city wall and walked along one of the wide main streets to the palace at the center of the city. I climbed

over the palace wall into a large outer courtyard.

The Emperor wanted me to see all the buildings in the palace and also his royal apartments. But since the space between the buildings was too narrow for me to place my feet on
the ground, I spent the next three days cutting
down the largest trees in the land and making
two very strong stools.

By standing on one stool in the large outer
courtyard and placing the second stool down
into a smaller courtyard, then lifting the first
one and repeating this process several times,
I was able to step over buildings, from one
stool to another, to get to the innermost court
where the royal apartments were located.

Once there, I lay down on my side and
brought my eyes up against the middle-story
windows of the palace. Inside, I saw the most
magnificent rooms I could ever imagine. The
young princes were there at play, with the Empress and her attendants watching over them.

I Brought My Eyes to the Palace Window.

This was a far different scene from other Lilliputian homes, where children weren't with their families. Instead, they were raised in nurseries and permitted to see their parents only twice a year, and then for only half an hour!

When the Empress saw me, or rather my eye, at her window, watching her and her children, she reached out her hand for me to kiss it. How honored I was to do so!

I was truly enjoying my freedom and the privileges the Emperor had granted me. I was allowed to cut down the largest trees in the royal park to make a table and chair for myself instead of eating on the ground. Over three hundred cooks prepared excellent meals for me and were amazed to see me eat a whole turkey or goose in one mouthful!

I was also given two hundred seamstresses who made new shirts for me, using my old one as a pattern, and three hundred tailors who used ladders to climb up and measure my body

She Reached Out Her Hand.

to make a new suit for me. Because the suit was made of small patches of cloth sewn together, it came out looking much like the patchwork quilts English ladies made as bed coverings.

Once I had my new clothes, I invited the Emperor, the Empress, and Flimnap, the Lord High Treasurer, to my home for dinner. I placed them all on my table in their royal chairs, which they had brought with them.

I ate a grand dinner, as if to show His Majesty how much I enjoyed his country's food. But as I did so, I noticed Flimnap frowning at me when the Emperor wasn't looking. "Is the Lord High Treasurer secretly my enemy?" I wondered.

I later heard that Flimnap used this dinner to complain to the Emperor that I had already cost the kingdom over a million *sprugs*, their most valuable gold coin. And he was advising His Majesty to send me away before the entire treasury was used up.

Looking Like a Patchwork Quilt

Flimnap was also foolish enough to be jealous of his wife's friendship with me. While his wife *did* visit me, it was always with her sister and her children, just as many of the other ladies of the Court did. I enjoyed having them sit in their coaches on my table while I answered their questions about English ladies' clothing and manners.

How ridiculous Flimnap's jealousy was—to think I could have romantic feelings for a woman as tall as my middle finger! But between his concern for the Emperor's treasury and this jealousy, he became my enemy and used his great influence on the Emperor to try to turn him against me.

The one friend I was certain of was Reldresal, the Emperor's trusted Private Secretary, who had done me many favors at Court. So I wasn't too surprised to see him ride up to my house one morning and ask for an hour of my time, which I was only too glad to give him.

"Would you care to have me lie down so you

Flimnap Became My Enemy.

can reach my ear, sir?" I asked him.

"No, that won't be necessary. I'd prefer it if you would hold me in your hand and lift me up," he replied.

Once I had him in my hand before my face, Reldresal explained, "I have come to make you aware of two dangerous situations Lilliput is facing. One is a violent political group here at home and the other is a threat of invasion from a powerful enemy abroad."

"I didn't know about any of this, sir," I said in surprise. "Please go on."

"As to the problem here at home, I must explain that there are two groups here in Lilliput, the *Tramecksan* and the *Slamecksan*. We can tell them apart by the heels on their shoes. Those who wear high heels obey the ancient rules of our land, but those in low heels are loyal to our Emperor and his new laws. Naturally, these Low-Heels hold all the important offices in our government."

"Can't they work out their problems among

"Hold Me in Your Hand."

themselves?"

"Both groups hate each other so much, they won't eat or drink together or talk to one another. Even though there are more Tramecksan than Slamecksan, our Low-Heels are more powerful right now because of the offices they hold. However, we fear that the prince, who is heir to the throne, might favor the Tramecksan for one of his shoes has a heel higher than the other. This is a sad state since it also makes him walk unevenly."

I looked at this little man strangely and realized that he was very serious about these two groups of people. I didn't say anything, but waited for him to go on.

Reldresal did. "In addition to this fighting within our own kingdom, we are now threatened with an invasion from the island of Blefuscu, another great empire as large and as powerful as ours. Blefuscu is just across a narrow channel from Lilliput."

"Are the Blefuscudians the same size as

I Looked at This Little Man.

you?"

"Yes, Man-Mountain, all the people in our universe are our size, not at all like you and the people you say live in your kingdom. You must understand that we doubt the existence of such a kingdom with giant creatures like yourself. We believe that you dropped from the moon or a star, because if this universe had more people like you, the food supply would be gone in a few moons."

"Well, I did *not* drop from the moon or any star. But enough about that now, Reldresal. Tell me why you're at war with Blefuscu."

"This war goes back thirty-six moons to a time when the Emperor's grandfather was a boy. The practice in our entire universe had always been to break eggs at the *big* end before eating them. When this young prince was doing just that, he happened to cut one of his fingers. This enraged his father, the Emperor, who then issued a decree stating that everyone had to break open their eggs at the *small*

"Tell Me Why You're at War."

end, or be severely punished."

"A law regarding breaking open eggs?" I gasped.

"Yes, and this angered the people of Blefuscu so much that they started a war over it. During these many moons, there have been six wars between our two kingdoms. One war resulted in an Emperor losing his crown; another ended with an Emperor losing his life. All told, eleven thousand people have been put to death—all because they defied that law and continued breaking open their eggs at the big end!"

"Eleven thousand put to death over breaking eggs!" I cried in disbelief.

"And to made matters worse during these wars, the Emperor of Blefuscu encouraged Lilliputian Big-Endians, those who broke their eggs at the big end, to continue defying their Emperor. He even helped them to escape and come to live in his kingdom."

"And this war that started thirty-six moons

"Put to Death Over Breaking Eggs!"

ago is still going on?"

"Yes. We win some and the Blefuscudians win some. We've lost forty large ships, a greater number of smaller ones, and thirty thousand of our best sailors and soldiers. But the Blefuscudian losses are said to be even greater than ours."

"Then why do you fear a new attack?"

"We just learned that the Blefuscudians have rebuilt their fleet, even larger than before, and they are preparing to attack."

"And why have you come to me with this news?" I asked.

"His Majesty knows how strong and brave you are. He is certain that you will be ready to risk your life by defending him and his kingdom against these invaders."

"I stand to serve His Majesty in any way I can. It's the least I can do to repay him for his kindness and hospitality."

And so I prepared to go to war!

"The Blefuscudians Have Rebuilt Their Fleet."

I Started Making Plans.

Chapter 6

The Hero Becomes a Villain!

After learning of this threat of attack, I stayed away from the coast so the Blefuscudians wouldn't see me. They didn't know of my existence, for all communication and trade between the two kingdoms had been forbidden.

I started making plans to capture the Blefuscudian fleet and sent for the Emperor's scouts to get the information I needed.

"Where is this new, large fleet right now?" I asked them.

"At anchor in the harbor across the channel, Man-Mountain," one scout replied. "They should set sail with the next good wind."

"And how deep is this channel?"

"When it's high tide, the water is seventy *glumgluffs* deep in the middle," a seaman replied. "But the rest is only fifty."

I did some quick arithmetic and figured that the deepest part of the channel was only six feet deep and the rest, a little over four feet.

Next, I hurried to the northeast coast, and lay down behind a hill to stay out of sight as much as possible. I took out my telescope to view the fleet and counted fifty warships and many transports.

Returning home, I gave orders to have long lengths of heavy cable and iron bars brought to me. I twisted three lengths of cable together to make them thicker and stronger, then tied the cable to the iron bars, which I wrapped in packs of three, bending one end into a hook.

Armed with fifty hooked cables, I returned to the coast an hour before high tide came in.

I Took Out My Telescope.

I left my jacket, shoes, and stockings on the shore and waded across until the water got too deep. Then I swam until my feet could touch bottom once again. This took less than a half an hour.

The enemy were so terrified when they saw me wade towards their fleet that thirty thousand sailors jumped off their warships and swam to shore. I immediately began hooking my cables onto the prows of the ships and tied the loose ends together in my hand. As I worked, my hands and face were attacked by thousands of arrows. Fearing severe damage to my eyes, I put on my glasses to protect myself.

Once all my cables were hooked on, I used my knife to cut their anchors. Then I easily pulled the fifty warships behind me across the channel.

Cries of grief and despair from the Blefuscudians reached my ears, but I was too busy towing their ships and pulling their arrows out

I Pulled the Warships Behind Me.

of my hands and face to be troubled about them.

The Emperor and his whole Court were standing on shore as I made my way across the channel. From where they stood, they could make out the fifty ships that fanned out in a semi-circle behind me, but they couldn't see me because I was walking in deep water up to my nose.

"Our Man-Mountain has drowned!" cried the Emperor. "And enemy ships are coming to attack us!"

Within minutes, though, the channel became shallower and I walked out of the water, holding up the cables for all the Lilliputians to see. I called out in a loud voice, "Long live the most powerful Emperor of Lilliput!"

How His Majesty praised me when I reached the shore! He even made me a *Nardac*, which is the highest title of honor awarded in the kingdom. But his next requests disturbed me.

The Emperor and Court Were On Shore.

"Man-Mountain, I wish you to bring the rest of the Blefuscudian ships to Lilliput. I wish to rule that land and destroy all the Big-Endians who fled there. Then I'll force the rest of the people to break open their eggs at the small end!"

"But, Your Majesty, that seems like a very harsh punishment," I protested. "I helped you by bringing their warships here, but I could never help you kill the Big-Endians or make slaves of the rest of the Blefuscudians."

The Emperor glared at me, then stormed away in anger. I knew then that he would never forgive me for refusing to help him carry out these unreasonable schemes. While many of his Council agreed with me, they were too frightened to oppose him. Others in the Council, for reasons I would never know, had chosen to become my enemy and they took advantage of this situation.

From that time on, these enemies spoke badly of me to the Emperor, who was eager to

The Emperor Stormed Away in Anger.

listen to them and eager to help them plot my destruction.

"How quickly His Majesty forgets the many services I did for him!" I reminded myself. "How greedy he is for power!"

About three weeks after I captured the Blefuscudian warships, six ambassadors and a train of five hundred people arrived from that island to ask for peace. Our Emperor agreed to a treaty that would naturally benefit him and Lilliput.

Since I was still officially welcome at Court, I was among the officials invited to greet the ambassadors. It seems that someone had secretly told them how I had spoken on their behalf to prevent the Emperor from attacking and enslaving their people.

The Head Ambassador praised me in his greeting. "We know how brave and strong you are, Man-Mountain. So, our Emperor has asked me to invite you to visit Blefuscu."

"I'd be delighted to do so before I return to

The Blefuscudians Arrive.

my country," I replied. "For I've heard many praises about your Emperor and the way he rules his kingdom."

Afterwards, I went to the Emperor of Lilliput to ask permission to visit Blefuscu. While he agreed to let me go, he did it in a rather cold and resentful manner. I couldn't understand this at first, but I soon learned that Flimnap and Bolgolam had convinced the Emperor that I had been using my conversations with the Blefuscudian ambassadors to complain about Lilliput.

However, it wasn't long after this that I had the opportunity to do what I thought was a great service to His Majesty. It happened late one night, when I was awakened by a hundred people banging at my door and shouting to me. "Hurry, Man-Mountain, hurry! You must come to the palace immediately!"

Several members of the Court made their way through the crowd and shouted, "We need your help. The Empress' apartment is on fire.

I Went to Ask Permission.

We have ladders against the walls and we're throwing buckets of water onto the fire, but we can't put it out."

I knew that their buckets were equal in size to a thimble and that a large burst of water was needed to put out a fire in such a large palace. So I ordered the crowd, "Leave at once and don't block the path from here to the sea and from the sea to the palace."

I immediately hurried to the sea and filled every inch of my mouth with water. Then I rushed to the palace and spit out the mouthful with such force that within three minutes the fire was completely extinguished. I was delighted to have saved that wonderful building from destruction.

I returned to my house without waiting for thanks from the Emperor. I was concerned, however, that he might be upset at the way I had put out the fire, since the laws of Lilliput make it a crime to spit anywhere near the palace. I later learned that although the Em-

Filling My Mouth With Sea Water

peror agreed to pardon me, the Empress was so enraged at what I had done that she moved to another building at the palace and swore that she would never return to the apartment I had spit on.

So, within a few weeks, my spitting had changed me from a hero to a villain!

The Empress Was Enraged.

In a Closed Coach

Chapter 7

Charged with Treason!

While I was preparing for my visit to Blefuscu, I had a secret visitor one night—it was a lord I had befriended when the Emperor became displeased with him. The lord came in a closed coach so he wouldn't be recognized.

I lifted him up, coach and all, and placed him on my table. He looked very worried as he climbed down and said, "I had to warn you, my friend. There have been secret Council meetings about you, and yesterday His Majesty made his decisions."

"Decisions about what?"

"Your fate! Skyresh Bolgolam has been so enraged since you captured the Blefuscudian fleet, something he could never do, that he has been plotting against you with Flimnap."

"But I was only following the Emperor's orders," I protested.

"I know that and so do many others. But those two have managed to convince the Council that you pose a danger to our kingdom and they've drawn up charges of treason against you. Because of the many favors you've done for me, it seemed only right that I risk my life to get a copy of those charges. I'll read them to you.

"Charge 1. There is a law in Lilliput that states spitting near the palace is an act of treason. The Man-Mountain maliciously defied that law by spitting water to put out a fire in the Empress' apartment.

"Charge 2. That after seizing fifty Blefuscudian warships, the Man-Mountain refused to seize the rest of the fleet, refused to help enslave

"Spitting Near the Palace Is Treason."

the people of that Empire, and refused to put to death all Big-Endians living there, all in defiance of orders given him by our most Kindly, Generous Majesty.

"Charge 3. That the Man-Mountain traitorously welcomed ambassadors from Blefuscu, knowing them to be servants of an Emperor who was recently our own Majesty's enemy.

"Charge 4. That the Man-Mountain is not behaving like a loyal subject by planning to make a voyage to Blefuscu, even though he has the Emperor's permission."

I sat on my chair, not knowing whether to laugh or take these charges seriously.

The lord put his paper down and explained, "The Emperor did point out to his Council the many services you had performed for him, but the Treasurer and High Admiral insisted that you be put to death in the most painful way, by setting fire to your house at night while you slept *and* by having an army of twenty thousand soldiers shoot you in the face and hands

To Laugh or Take It Seriously?

with poisoned arrows *and* by having your servants splash poisoned juice on your shirts and sheets to make you tear at your skin and have a torturous death!"

I realized now this was nothing to laugh at, and I listened as the lord went on.

"His Majesty wanted to spare your life and, knowing Reldresal was your friend, he asked his Private Secretary for an opinion."

"Yes, yes, I'm certain that helped," I said with great relief.

"Not so quickly, my friend. Reldresal did agree that your crimes were great, but he advised the Emperor to spare your life."

"Good! Good!" I exclaimed, smiling.

"Good? Hardly! Reldresal recommended that His Majesty show mercy and prove he was a fair and generous ruler by just putting out your eyes and not killing you. That way, you could be led around by his ministers and your strength would still be useful to him."

"I can't believe this!" I gasped in shock.

Poisoned Arrows and Poisoned Juice!

"But the High Admiral wouldn't hear of it. He said putting your eyes out was too easy a punishment. Besides, you could drown the entire palace with mouthfuls of water if you wanted to. No, he insisted on death! And the Treasurer agreed, arguing that the treasury couldn't go on supporting you and that you'd probably eat more once your eyes were out!"

"And what was their final decision?"

"The Emperor still refused to put you to death, and asked Reldresal again if he had any other punishment that could be added to putting your eyes out. The Secretary thought a while, then suggested slowly cutting back on your food supply. The treasury would be saving money and you'd grow weaker and weaker until you died."

"And what do they plan to do with my body when I was dead?"

"The Emperor would have five thousand men cut away your flesh, cart it away, and bury it in a distant part of the land. But he

"You Could Drown the Entire Palace!"

would leave your skeleton behind for the people to admire."

"And how was this wonderful suggestion received?" I asked with sarcasm.

"Everyone agreed to this idea. And they also agreed to keep it a secret."

"And when am I to receive this delightful news?"

"In three days. The Secretary will come here to read you the charges and the punishment. He will assure you that your eyes would be put out with expert skill by His Majesty's own surgeons, who will shoot sharp-pointed arrows into your eyes."

With that, the lord wished me luck and returned to the city as secretly as he had come.

I sat for a long while talking to myself. "Should I risk a trial and attempt to prove my innocence? . . . No, I'm still free and strong enough to crush this entire empire and everyone in it. . . . Yet, I've taken an oath to be loyal to the Emperor and protect his kingdom."

The Lord Returned to the City.

Finally, after several hours, I made a decision. "To save my eyes, and of course my life, I won't wait for the Secretary to come. I'll leave on my visit to the Emperor of Blefuscu sooner than I planned. In fact, I'll leave today!"

When the sun rose that morning, I sent a messenger to the palace, advising the Emperor that with his permission, I was leaving for Blefuscu. I didn't wait for an answer, but gathered my belongings and hurried to the northeast coast of the island. There, I seized a large warship from the fleet, tied a cable to its prow, and lifted up the anchor. I put my clothes and my bed cover into the ship and began to pull it along, as I waded into the water, then swam across the channel.

I Seized a Large Warship.

Guides Climbed Into My Hands.

Chapter 8

Blefuscu and Freedom

It wasn't long before I arrived at the royal port of Blefuscu and was given a warm welcome. Two guides climbed up into my hands and led me to the gates of the capital city, where I waited until they announced me.

The Emperor and the Royal Family came out to greet me. His Majesty got down from his horse and the Empress from her coach. No one seemed frightened of me in any way. I lay down on the ground to kiss their hands.

"I have come here, Your Majesty, with the permission of the Emperor of Lilliput, to meet you and offer you my services."

I said nothing of my disgrace back in Lilliput, which I wasn't supposed to know about anyway. I was just thankful to be free of that kingdom after a stay of nine months and thirteen days, and I accepted the warm welcome from the Blefuscudians.

There was no building in this kingdom big enough to house me, so I spread my cover on the ground and wrapped myself in it to go to sleep.

I spent the first few days exploring the island. On the third day, while walking along the northeast coast, I spotted in the distant sea something that looked like an overturned boat. I took off my shoes and stockings, and waded out towards it as the tide pushed it towards me.

"It *is* a boat!" I cried with joy. "A boat *my* size, not Blefuscudian size. It seems to be a longboat from a sailing ship. Perhaps it was tossed loose by a storm."

In the Distant Sea

I immediately headed back to shore and to the Emperor's palace, where I explained to His Majesty what I had seen. Then I begged,

"Your Majesty, would you be kind enough to lend me twenty of the tallest ships that were left in your fleet and three thousand seamen?"

My request was granted, and I hurried to prepare some ropes to take back to the long-boat with me. At the same time, the fleet was sailing around to that side of the island. Meanwhile, the tide had brought the overturned longboat in closer to shore, but I still had to swim out and push it to shallower water.

Once I was able to stand, I had the Blefus-cudian seamen toss me the ropes, which I tied to the longboat. With the ships pulling and me pushing, we brought the boat closer to shore. Then, with two thousand men working with ropes and pulleys, we managed to turn the boat right side up. How delighted I was to discover that it was barely damaged!

I spent the next ten days making paddles,

I Prepared Some Ropes.

then brought my boat around to the port. The Emperor was at the front of the crowd on shore, gaping at the size of the boat.

"Your Majesty," I said, bowing humbly, "it seems that I've been fortunate to have this boat drift my way, for it's exactly what I need to return to my own country. I'm just as fortunate to have such a kind and generous Emperor as yourself to help me bring it here to port. Now, I need one last favor."

"Speak, Man-Mountain," said the Emperor with a smile. "I will grant you whatever is in my power to give."

"I'll need provisions for my voyage and, of course, your permission to leave."

"You shall have both, my friend."

"And what of the message you received three days ago from the Emperor of Lilliput?" I asked, knowing that the Lilliputians would become suspicious when I didn't return in several days, and try to get me back.

"The envoy did arrive to inform me of your

The Emperor Gaped at the Size of the Boat.

crimes and to demand that I return you, tied hand and foot, to be punished as a traitor. If I didn't, he threatened that it would be considered an act of war!"

The Emperor of Blefuscu was smiling as he went on. "Please don't worry, for I sent the envoy back just today with the friendliest of words to His Majesty. I also informed him what he already knew—that it would be quite impossible for us to tie *you* hand and foot and get you to Lilliput if you didn't want to go. I also reminded him that even though you captured our fleet, you were still very helpful in making peace between us."

"And did you tell him I plan to leave?"

"Yes. I assured him that both our kingdoms would soon have nothing to fear from you and no longer have the burden of feeding and clothing you, for you had found a boat and would be heading back to your own land."

"You're very kind, Your Majesty, and I do thank you."

"An Act of War!"

"But hear me out, Man-Mountain. I'm prepared to offer you my protection if you would agree to stay here and serve me."

While I believed the Emperor to be sincere, my experience in Lilliput had taught me not to trust *any* ruler ever again. So, although I couldn't tell him that, I did explain, "Your Majesty, I do appreciate your trust in me, but I really couldn't be the cause of another war between your two kingdoms now that you're finally at peace."

With my mind made up and the Emperor's help, five hundred men were put to work making sails for my boat. Then, a thousand carpenters helped me make the masts, oars, and cables. For an anchor, I used a large rock I found on the beach.

At the end of a month, everything was ready. The boat was loaded with the meat of a hundred oxen and three hundred sheep, and enough bread and drink for my voyage. I took six cows and two bulls, and many ewes and

Five Hundred Men Put to Work Making Sails.

rams, with the hope of breeding them back in England. And to feed them on board, I had bags of hay and corn.

I went to the palace to bid farewell to the Emperor and the Royal Family. As His Majesty offered his hand, I lay down on my face to kiss it. He then presented me with a full-length, life-size painting of himself and fifty tiny pouches, each containing two hundred *sprugs*, their gold coins.

I would have been delighted to take some little people with me, but this was not permitted, even if any of them had wanted to go. Still, His Majesty felt it was necessary to have my pockets searched just the same.

So it was that on September 24, 1701, at six o'clock in the morning, I set sail. My pocket compass served me well as I headed north the entire day. By evening, I neared an island that appeared to be uninhabited. Feeling safe, I dropped anchor near the shore and slept very well.

Fifty Tiny Pouches of Gold Coins

The following morning, I continued heading north, then veered to the northeast. At three in the afternoon of the following day, I spotted a sail heading southeast. With the help of the wind, I quickly followed until the ship sighted me and I joyously recognized its British flag.

At six that evening, I gathered my belongings and my tiny animals from the longboat and climbed aboard the ship, a British merchant vessel returning from Japan.

When I told the story of my adventures to the captain, he thought I was mad and told his officers, "Whatever dangers this man has faced have caused him to lose his mind!"

"I haven't lost my mind, sir!" I argued. "Look! Here's proof." And I took the tiny cattle and sheep out of my pocket and placed them on the table before me.

"Good Lord!" cried the astonished captain. "You *are* telling the truth!"

As further proof, I showed him the tiny bags of gold the Emperor had given me and his full-

I Spotted a Sail

length picture.

Our trip back to England was very pleasant. The captain was eager to help me care for my tiny cattle and even gave me some of his best biscuits, which I crushed into a powder and mixed with water to feed them. To show my thanks when we docked in England, I gave him a cow and a pregnant sheep.

My feet touched British soil on April 13, 1702, just under three years from the time I'd left. I stayed with my family for two months and made a large amount of money displaying my cattle, then much more by finally selling them. I bought a fine house for my family and gave them enough money to live on for several years.

As always, I was too restless to stay on land for long. So, I signed on board a merchant ship heading for the coast of India.

A Fine House for My Family

Twenty Days of Violent Winds

Chapter 9

Stranded in a Land of Giants

On the 20th of June, 1702, I set sail on the *Adventure,* heading south around Europe and down the coast of Africa toward the Cape of Good Hope. We stopped there to take on fresh water, but discovered a leak in the ship. Repairs took many months and continued into winter, so we couldn't resume our voyage until March of 1703.

As we turned the Cape and headed north, past the island of Madagascar and toward the Arabian Sea, we ran into twenty days of violent winds. Weeks of calm weather followed, but the captain knew the weather in these seas and warned us to be ready for an even more violent storm, a monsoon. It hit us the very next day!

We immediately took down the sails and fastened down all the guns on deck. Days upon days of strong winds blew us off course. I thought we were being blown east, and even the most experienced men on board couldn't tell what part of the world we were in.

The ship was sturdy and the crew in good health, but we were badly in need of water. On June 16th, a seaman on the top mast spied land, and the following day a huge island loomed before us. We headed towards a small cove, but had to drop anchor outside it because the water was filled with dangerous, sharp-pointed rocks.

Twelve of us went ashore in a longboat to search for a river or a spring where we could get drinking water. We separated on shore and went off in different directions.

A Huge Island Loomed Before Us.

After an hour of trudging over rocky, barren land and finding no water and no inhabitants, I started back towards the longboat. Reaching a hill above the cove, I was shocked to see the eleven other crewmen already in the boat, rowing for their lives towards the ship.

"Wait! Wait for me!" I shouted, but they paid no attention to me.

The next moment, I saw the reason why. A huge creature, *sixty feet tall*, was walking after them into the sea, walking almost as fast as they were rowing. He was taking long steps in water up to his knees, but the sharp-pointed rocks prevented him from overtaking the long-boat.

"Good grief!" I cried as I turned and ran. My only thought was to escape. I kept running until I found a steep hill, from which I could get a better view of the island I was on. As I looked around, I saw that the land was culti-vated with fields of hay and corn . . . but with stalks that were growing from twenty to forty

"Wait! Wait For Me!"

feet tall!

I set off on a path through a field of corn that towered forty feet over my head. When I came to the end of the field, I found it fenced in with hedges over one hundred feet high and trees so tall that I couldn't even judge how high up they went.

A stone stile led from one field to the next, with four steps to reach the top. I couldn't climb this stile because each sep was six feet high. I was trying to find an opening in the hedge when I discovered another giant of the same size as the one who was chasing the longboat.

Terrified, I hid myself in the corn, as sounds seemed to come from the giant. But they were so loud and so high up that they seemed more like thunder than words. Within moments, seven more giants came towards him, each carrying a reaping-hook. They immediately began cutting down the stalks of corn all around me. I began to run blindly, looking des-

Corn Towering Forty Feet High

perately for someplace to hide, someplace where I wouldn't be squashed to death under a giant's foot or cut in two with his reaping-hook. Finally, I jumped into a trench between two ridges of dirt and tried to hide under some stalks that were already cut down and laying there.

Frightened and grief-stricken, I whispered goodbye prayers to my wife and family. I asked their forgiveness for having been so foolish as to have gone off on this voyage against their wishes and against the advice of my friends and relations.

I Jumped into a Trench.

The Huge Creature Stopped in His Tracks.

Chapter 10

Saved from Children and Rats!

My sorrowful whispers were interrupted by the crunch of a huge foot about to come down on top of me. I screamed as loudly as my lungs would let me, "STOP! NO! PLEASE! I'M DOWN HERE!"

The huge creature stopped in his tracks and looked around him on the ground until he caught sight of me. He knelt down and studied me, much as I would have looked down to see a strange insect on the ground.

Then he reached down and picked me up, gripping me across my waist between his thumb and middle finger. He slowly brought me up to his eye level to study me.

Hoping and praying that all he wanted to do was look, I decided not to struggle, even though I was dangling in the air sixty feet above the ground. I raised my eyes towards heaven, clasped my hands, and whispered some prayers, as if to show him I was a peace-loving creature. He seemed pleased with my gestures even though he didn't understand the words I was speaking.

When his fingers began hurting me, I began to groan and shed tears, pointing to my sides which were being pinched. He seemed to understand what I was trying to say, for he lifted up the flap on his jacket pocket and gently put me inside. Then he ran to bring me to his master, who was the farmer I had first seen in the field.

The farmer stood me in the palm of his left hand and, with a piece of straw the size of an Englishman's cane, he lifted up the flap of my

He Brought Me to Eye Level.

jacket. "Now, what kind of covering has Nature given to this strange creature?" he seemed to ask. Then he blew my hair aside. "And what does its face look like?"

When he still couldn't figure what I was, he gently put me on the ground on all fours. But I stood up and walked slowly back and forth to show him I wasn't a four-legged creature and I wasn't trying to run away.

By now, all the other workers had gathered around me in a circle to watch me move. I took off my hat and bowed low to the farmer. Then I took a purse of gold from my pocket and placed it in his open palm. He brought the pouch up close to his eyes, but couldn't figure out what it was. He jabbed it with a pin to see if it moved, but it didn't.

I signaled to him to lay his hand flat on the ground, which he did. I then opened the purse and poured all the gold into his palm. He wet the tip of his little finger with his tongue and dabbed at his palm to pick up some of the gold,

154

"What Does Its Face Look Like?"

but he had no idea what it was. He signaled me to put the gold back into the pouch, which I did.

The farmer was convinced by now that I was a sane, thinking creature, not some insect or animal newly dug up from the earth. He spoke many words to me, but they came out sounding like booming thunder.

While I answered as loudly as I could, in as many different languages as I knew, we still couldn't understand each other.

In a while, he sent his servants back to work, then spread his handkerchief on the ground and signaled for me to step into it. This wasn't difficult, for the cloth was only one foot thick. I feared I might fall if I stood straight up, so I stretched out full length on the handkerchief and was wrapped up and carried to the farmhouse.

The farmer gently placed me on a table and showed me to his wife, who took one look at me and screamed. I was even more frightened,

Wrapped Up and Carried to the Farmhouse

however, of the table itself, which was thirty feet up from the floor!

When lunch time came, the farmer's wife brought in a dish of meat twenty-four feet across. Two of the family's three children came to the table, a boy of ten and a girl of nine, and watched as their mother mashed a bit of meat for me on a small plate and added some crumbled bread.

I bowed to the woman as my way of saying thanks. Then I took a knife and fork from my pocket and began to eat. The entire family watched with delight. When I was offered a drink from the smallest cup they had, I barely managed to lift it with both my hands, since it held two gallons. But it was a welcome drink, tasting much like cider.

The farmer then motioned for me to come close to his plate. As I made my way there, trying to avoid platters and glasses and silver, which were like mountains in my path, I stumbled against a crust of bread and fell flat on

The Entire Family Watched Me Eat.

my face. But I wasn't hurt and got up immediately.

I met greater trouble, however, when I passed by the plate of the farmer's ten-year-old son, who seized me by the legs and lifted me high in the air above his head.

The farmer came to my rescue and snatched me from him. He then gave the boy a hard slap on the hand and ordered him, "Leave the table at once! I'll punish you when I finish my meal."

"Please, master," I begged, falling to my knees and talking in as much sign language as I could. "He's only a child. I'm certain he didn't mean to hurt me."

I did this actually because I didn't want to make an enemy of the child, who might get back at me when his father wasn't around.

After dinner, a servant brought in the family's one-year-old baby. When he saw me, he reached out his hand for this new toy and let out a scream when he couldn't reach me. To quiet him, the mother picked me up and placed

Greater Trouble!

me gently in his hand. The baby squeezed me tightly across the middle, then and immediately put my head in his mouth.

I let out such a terrifying roar that the baby dropped me. If the mother hadn't spread her apron to catch me, I surely would have broken my neck! Her kindness continued after dinner when, seeing me yawn and start to close my eyes, she put me on her bed and covered me with a clean, white handkerchief, which was large enough to hang as a sail on the largest warship in the British fleet.

I slept for two hours and awoke feeling refreshed. I opened my eyes and looked at the bed on which I had slept—it was sixty feet wide! I looked down—it was twenty-four feet above the floor!

I didn't have too much time to study the room, for I was suddenly attacked from both sides by two giant rats, the size of large dogs. One came at my face, while the other jumped on my neck. I quickly drew my sword and

The Mother Reached Out to Catch Me.

ripped open the belly of one rat before he could sink his teeth into my throat. Seeing his comrade fall dead, the other rat turned to flee, but not before I managed to cut deeply into his back as he ran.

I got up then and walked around on the bed to catch my breath. I looked at the dead rat and saw that its tail alone was six feet long!

When the farmer's wife came into the room a while later, she was horrified to see blood all over the bed and all over me. Fearing that I had been injured, she picked me up in her hand and brought me close to her face. But I smiled at her and pointed to the dead rat on the bed.

She sighed with relief, then called for her maid to throw away the rat and clean up the room while she took me out to her garden for some fresh air.

Its Tail Was Six Feet Long!

My "Little" Nurse

Chapter 11

A Performing Splacknuck

The nine-year-old daughter in the family stood forty feet tall, which was considered short for her age! She was a very responsible child who was to become my best friend and protector. *Glumdalclitch*, or "little nurse," which I named her, had many talents which would benefit me all the time I spent in this land. Without her care and affection, I doubt that I would have survived.

My little nurse named me *Grildrig*, a name that meant "dwarf" or "pixie." She fixed up her doll's cradle for her little pixie to sleep in and hung it from a shelf so the rats couldn't get to me. She was skillful at sewing clothes for her dolls and soon began making shirts for me. She also took on the role of my teacher. Through her efforts, I quickly began to understand and speak the language of this land, which I learned was called Brobdingnag.

She also told me what people were saying about me. "Everyone calls you a tame and gentle little creature who obeys all the commands of our people when they ask you to do something."

I explained to her, "Your father is my master, so I must please him. Why, just this morning, a neighboring farmer, an old man, came by, and your father put me on display on the table. He told me to draw my sword, then sheath it. I did just that, then bowed and asked the man how he was feeling, in the language you taught me. The man put on his glasses to see me better and leaned very close to me. His eyes looked like two moons shining

She Made Shirts for Me.

into a bedroom window, and I began to laugh. This angered the old man, especially when your father began to laugh too."

"I know that man. He's not very pleasant and is said to be a stingy miser as well."

"Well, he then went to the other side of the room with your father and they spoke in whispers, pointing to me several times during their conversation."

The next day, Glumdalclitch learned what that secret conversation was all about and she came to me in tears, holding me against her chest as she spoke. "Oh, my little Grildrig, today is market-day in the neighboring town, and my father is planning to put you on display and charge people for having a look at you. I think it's terrible! Some of these rude people could break one of your arms or legs or even squeeze you to death. Besides, you're such a modest person. I can't bear to think what an insult this is."

"Thank you for your concern, my dear nurse.

She Was In Tears.

But I'm a stranger in your country and really must behave with all politeness. And your father *is* my master."

That day, the farmer put me in a box with air holes and a door cut into it. Glumdalclitch made sure she put her doll's quilt on the bottom of the box to give me something soft to lie on before she took her place on a cushion behind my box on the horse. Still, I was very badly shaken during the half-hour ride to town. Since the horse covered forty feet with each step, I felt as if I were on a ship, rising and falling in a violent storm at sea.

We arrived at an inn, where the farmer hired a crier and told him, "Announce to the townspeople that I am displaying a strange creature that resembles a *splacknuck*. However, my animal has a body like a human's and can speak real words and do hundreds of entertaining tricks."

The farmer set me down on a table in the inn's largest room. My little nurse sat on a low

The Farmer Put Me in a Box.

stool close by to take care of me and explain what I was to do. The farmer was allowing only thirty people to enter the room at a time to view me.

Glumdalclitch had me walk around the table, answer questions she asked, speak words of welcome to the visitors, drink toasts to their health from a thimble filled with wine, and draw my sword to demonstrate fencing as it was done in England.

I repeated this over and over twelve times that day, for eight hours without a stop, until I was half-dead with weariness and anger. People were close to breaking down the doors to get in as they heard of the wonderful performance from earlier visitors.

No one was allowed to touch me, orders the farmer gave simply to keep me unharmed and earning money rather than to protect me. But a mischievous boy managed to throw a nut at my head. Since nuts in this land are the size of large pumpkins, my head could have been

To Demonstrate Fencing

split open if his aim had been good. However, I did get the satisfaction of seeing him beaten and thrown out of the room.

The farmer showed me off again the following market-day, as well as for visitors at his home. He was becoming so greedy that even at his farmhouse, he charged visitors to see me. He forced them to pay what he would usually earn from a room full of thirty people, even if there were only five or six.

This went on day after day for two months, at home or in town on market-day. The only time I had to rest was Wednesday, which was the Brobdingnag sabbath.

Seeing how valuable I was, the farmer then decided to travel throughout the kingdom to show me off. Our first destination was the capital city, about three thousand miles from his house.

Glumdalclitch rode behind her father on his horse, carrying me tied around her waist in a special traveling box she had built for me. She

Our Destination Was the Capital.

had placed her doll's bed in it for me and lined the box with the silkiest and softest cloths she could find.

For two weeks, we traveled through twenty large towns and many more small villages, stopping anywhere, even at private homes, where people would pay well to see the splack-nuck perform.

Along the way, my little nurse often complained of aches and pains so her father would stop to rest. But she was actually making up excuses to stop and let me out of my box to get some air or exercise, or simply to see the view.

On October 26th, we arrived in the capital city, *Lorbrulgrud*. The farmer rented a room at an inn on the main street, near the royal palace, then had announcements about my performance printed and distributed.

I was shown ten times a day on a huge, sixty-foot table to captivated audiences. By now, I was able to speak their language quite well and understood everything that was said

Twenty Towns and Many Villages

to me. My little nurse was even teaching me to read, which was how we spent many hours on our long journeys.

This demanding schedule of ten performances a day began to affect my health. But the more money the farmer was making, the more he wanted. And the more I performed, the weaker and thinner I became. Seeing that I was beginning to look like a skeleton, the farmer decided that he'd better get the most use out of me before I died and his source of easy money came to an end!

Looking Like a Skeleton

"You May Kiss My Little Finger."

Chapter 12

The Queen's Favorite

While the farmer was trying to figure out how to make the most money from me before I died, a messenger arrived at the inn ordering the farmer to bring me to the Queen.

He obeyed immediately and took Glumdalclitch along with us. When he placed me on the table before the Queen, I fell to my knees.

"Your Majesty, may I have the honor of kissing your royal foot?" I pleaded.

The Queen smiled down at me and shook her head. "Certainly not, little visitor. But you may kiss my little finger."

I embraced that finger with both my arms and brought my lips respectfully to its tip.

The Queen asked me many questions about my country and my travels, which I answered as best I could.

Then she surprised me with her next question. "Do you think you could be happy living at Court?"

I made a deep bow in the direction of the farmer and explained, "I belong to the man who brought me here, but if I were free to make a choice, I'd be proud to serve Her Majesty for life."

She then turned to the farmer and asked, "Will you sell me this slave?"

"Certainly! At a good price, Your Majesty. Perhaps a thousand pieces of gold." And to himself, the farmer chuckled, "Since the splacknuck will probably be dead in a month, this will be an excellent deal for me."

The Queen accepted the farmer's price and had the gold brought to him immediately.

"Could You Be Happy at Court?"

I then bowed again to Her Majesty. "Now that I'm your slave, I must beg you for one more thing—to permit Glumdalclitch, who has cared for me and knows me so well, to continue as my nurse and teacher."

The Queen agreed and looked to Glumdalclitch, who was overjoyed, and to the farmer as he nodded his consent.

"It will be to my advantage to have my daughter in such good favor at the Court," the greedy farmer thought to himself as he bowed to the Queen and then to me.

I returned his false smile with a cold stare and the slightest of bows as he left.

The Queen noticed my coldness and asked, "Why did you look at your master that way?"

I explained, "While I owe him my life for not killing me when he found me, he's been more than repaid with the money he's made by forcing me to entertain his audiences day and night for months. As a result, my health has suffered. If he didn't think that I was close to

The Queen Agreed.

death, he'd never have sold me to you, Gracious Queen. But I'm certain that with your protection, I'll recover soon."

"What a delightful and intelligent creature you are!" she exclaimed. "I must take you to meet the King at once." She lifted me in the palm of her hand and carried me along as I lay stretched out on my stomach.

Upon seeing me, His Majesty gave the Queen a scowl and demanded, "Since when have you become so fond of splacknucks that you carry them around with you?"

The Queen simply smiled at her husband as she stood me on his desk. "Tell His Majesty who you are and where you've come from," she said to me.

I did so as best I could. Glumdalclitch, who was standing at the door, confirmed everything I said about my life from the time I arrived at her father's house.

The King studied me for a while, then announced, "When I first saw you walk, I decid-

"To the King at Once!"

ed you were some sort of mechanical doll. Then when I heard you speak, and speak so sensibly, I decided that perhaps you were simply a dwarf. But you're even smaller than the Queen's favorite dwarf, who stands thirty feet high. So, I'm forced to believe everything you've told me about your country and the millions of small creatures like yourself who live there."

I bowed to the King, who then ordered that special care be given me. "And see to it that his little nurse stays with him always and that she has her own servants too."

The Queen ordered her furniture-maker to build a box what would serve as a bedroom for me to use not only at the palace, but for traveling as well. Within three weeks, that bedroom box was ready. It was twelve feet square, and had softly quilted walls, closets, windows, a bed, a table, chairs, a cabinet, and a door with a lock. All my furniture was screwed to the floor to prevent any damage while we were

A Bedroom and Traveling Box

traveling. The outside of my box had a ring at the top for lifting it and hooks on one side to attach it to a rider's belt when I was carried about on horseback.

The Queen also had her seamstresses make me bed linens and clothes of the finest silks in the kingdom. She became so fond of me that she wouldn't dine without me in front of her on the table. I had my own small table and chair set up there, along with an entire of set of silver plates and eating utensils. The Queen would put a piece of meat on my dish and watch with delight as I cut and ate it myself.

On Wednesdays, their Sabbath, the King and Queen dined together with all the princes and princesses. At these dinners, I was placed in front of His Majesty, and we spent many hours talking about the countries of Europe, their laws, their government, systems of education, manners, and religion.

While the lords and ladies of the Court liked me, I soon learned that the Queen's dwarf,

My Own Table and Silver

who was jealous of my popularity, had become my enemy. His taunts didn't bother me, so he resorted to attacking me when no one was looking. First, he picked me up at the table, squeezed my legs together, and wedged me up to my waist inside a round marrow bone on the Queen's plate. For this, he got a whipping, which stopped only when I pleaded for mercy for him.

Another time, he dropped me into a large bowl of cream, then ran away. If I hadn't been such a good swimmer and if Glumdalclitch hadn't spotted me from the other end of the table and pulled me out, I might have drowned! I swallowed about a quart of cream and ruined a good suit of clothes. The dwarf was whipped soundly again. But this time, I had no desire to defend him and didn't protest when he was banished from Court.

He Dropped Me in a Large Bowl of Cream.

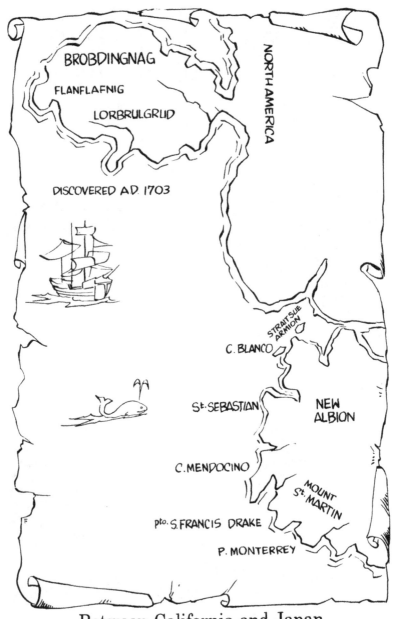

Between California and Japan

Attack of the Giant Animals!

Brobdingnag, I learned, formed a peninsula six thousand miles long and five thousand miles wide off the western coast of America. It's an area between California and Japan which British mapmakers have declared contained nothing but ocean. Down the length of the peninsula runs a ridge of mountains thirty miles high, with volcanoes at the top.

The kingdom contains fifty-one cities, a hundred walled towns, and even more small villages. The capital, Lorbrulgrud, with 80,000 houses, is divided in two by a river running through it. The palace's many buildings spread out for seven miles around, and its rooms are two hundred forty feet high.

I got to see the city in a coach that was given to Glumdalclitch for her own use. Although I was always carried about in my box, my little nurse often took me out to see the houses and people and to let the people see me and talk to me. On those occasions when I accompanied the King and Queen on a royal visit on horseback, my box was buckled to the waist of a trusted servant. A cushion was placed below the box and a hammock hung inside it so I wouldn't be tossed about by the galloping of a sixty-foot-high horse.

The Queen appreciated my interest in the palace library and gave me permission to borrow any books I chose. She had her carpenter build a kind of moving ladder for me in Glumdalclitch's room. It was twenty-five feet high, with steps fifty feet across.

The book I chose to read was propped up

Permission to Read Books

against the wall and the ladder propped up against the open page. I would climb up the ladder and, starting at the top left of the page, walk to the right, then back to the left, slowly going down the ladder until I came to the bottom of the page. I repeated the same procedure on the facing page, then turned to the next one, using both my hands on the thick, stiff paper that measured twenty feet across.

The Queen always enjoyed hearing me talk of my sea voyages, and she asked me one day, "Would you like to do some sailing or rowing perhaps, for pleasure or exercise?"

"Certainly, Your Majesty," I replied. "But there's no vessel small enough in Brobdingnag for me to manage."

"If you design one, I'll have it built and provide a place for you to sail it in."

Ten days later, I had a boat large enough to hold me and eight of my friends, if I had any of them here with me. It had a mast and sails and several oars. The boat was put into a

I Had a Boat.

wooden trough three hundred feet long, fifty feet wide and eight feet deep. I often rowed in it as the Queen and her ladies sat watching and praising my skills in maneuvering the vessel. When I wanted to sail, they used their fans to create strong winds or' ordered their pages to blow on my sails to move them with their breath.

While this pastime gave me much pleasure, it also was the cause of an accident that almost cost me my life. One of the servants whose job it was to refill my trough with fresh water every three days didn't notice a frog slip out of his pail and into the trough. Once my boat and I were placed in the trough, the frog hopped up onto the boat and began hopping backwards and forwards over me. This tilted the boat dangerously and covered me with its disgusting slime.

Seeing this attack, Glumdalclitch ran to rescue me. But I held her off, preferring to beat back my attacker with my oars, which I man-

Their Fans Created Strong Winds.

aged to do successfully.

But a frog wasn't the greatest danger I faced in Brobdingnag. That came from a monkey that belonged to a palace worker.

It happened one day when my little nurse went off on a visit to her family. She had locked me safely in her room, but since the weather was very warm and she wanted me to have enough air, she left her bedroom window open, along with those in my little box.

I was sitting quietly at my table when I heard and saw a monkey the size of an elephant bounce in the window and begin to leap up and down around the room. When he saw my box, he leaped towards it for a closer look, peeking curiously into my door and all my windows. I jumped up from the table and ran to the farthest corner of the room. I wasn't thinking too clearly or else I would have had the sense to hide under my bed.

When the monkey spied me, he began chattering and grinning, then reached his paw in-

A Monkey the Size of an Elephant

side the door and grabbed me. Although he was squeezing me very hard, he didn't seem to want to harm me. Instead, he cradled me in his right front foot, just the way a mother cradles an infant in her arms when she's about to nurse, and began stroking my face very gently.

Suddenly, the bedroom door opened. Glumdalclitch took a step inside the room, then froze. She let out a horrible scream as she ran towards us. The frightened monkey leaped up to the window and out onto the ledge. Walking on three legs and holding me in his fourth, he climbed up to the roof.

By now, my little nurse's screams had sent the entire palace into an uproar. Servants ran for ladders, while hundreds of Brobdingnagians shouted from the courtyard below. Meanwhile, the monkey sat calmly at the edge of the roof, still holding me in one paw and cramming some dirt and food into my mouth with another.

But when he saw men climbing up ladders

He Cradled Me in His Right Front Foot.

and surrounding him, the monkey decided to make his escape. Lucky for me, he dropped me onto a roof tile before he leaped away.

I sat there for a while, fearing I'd be blown off the roof by the wind or that I'd get dizzy and fall. But a brave footman reached me before that happened and carried me down safely in the pocket of his shirt.

I was nearly choked with the filthy garbage the monkey had tried to stuff down my throat, but my dear nurse picked it out of my mouth with a needle and gave me a drink. My body was weak and bruised from the monkey's squeezing, and I had to stay in bed for two weeks until my strength returned.

The King and Queen came to visit me often during those weeks and assured me that they had issued orders banning all monkeys from the palace and its surrounding gardens.

A Brave Footman Reached Me.

Not a Day Went By

Chapter 14

An Unexpected Escape

During the two years I had been in Brobd-ingnag, not a day went by without my hoping that I would escape and return home, even though I had no idea of how I would accomplish that. The ship in which I had arrived was the first ever seen in that land, and none had been sighted since. The King had given orders that if ever another one came close to their coast, it was to be brought ashore and its crew and passengers carried to the palace. His idea was to find a wife for me so I could raise a family and stay in his kingdom. But the thought of having children who would be kept in cages like tame birds was hateful to me! Besides, I could never forget my dear wife and children back in England.

As my third year in Brobdingnag began, I was unexpectedly given the chance to escape. Glumdalclitch and I were invited to accompany the King and Queen on a trip to their summer palace near the sea in Flanflasnic, in the southern part of the kingdom. The trip was long and tiring, and I came down with a slight cold. But my dear little nurse became so ill, she had to stay in bed.

Bring so close to the sea, I was filled with thoughts of escape every waking minute. Before I could make any plans, I had to see what the coastline looked like. So, I pretended to feel sicker than I really was and asked the Queen's permission to go to the shore, where I might breathe in the fresh sea air.

I was given permission and put in charge of a trusted page who had cared for me in the

Glumdalclitch Was Sick in Bed.

past. Glumdalclitch, however, burst into tears at the thought of someone else caring for me, and she gave him strict orders as to what he was to do and not do. It almost seemed as if she had a premonition, a feeling that something would happen to me.

The page carried me in my box to the rocks on the shore, where I ordered him to put me down. I raised one of my windows and looked sadly out to sea. Feeling a little sick, I told him that I was going to take a nap in my hammock. He closed my window to keep out the cold sea air and left me to my rest.

From that point on, I can only guess that the boy may have gone off to look for shells or birds' eggs and left my box alone on the rocks, for the next thing I knew, I suddenly found myself awakened by a violent pull on the carrying ring at the top of my box. Then I felt the box raised very high in the air, and carried forward at great speed.

Clinging to my hammock, I called out at the

Looking Sadly Out to Sea

top of my lungs, but there was no reply. I looked towards my windows, but saw only clouds and sky. Above me, I heard a noise like the flapping of wings and I suddenly realized what had happened. "Oh, no!" I gasped. "Some eagle has the ring of my box in his beak, and he probably intends to drop it on a rock, like eagles do with turtles to crack open their shells before eating them!"

Soon the noise and flutter of the eagle's wings increased, and my box was tossed up and down like a signpost on a windy day. Suddenly, I heard several bangs against the eagle's body, then felt my box dropping. I was dropping with such incredible speed that I nearly lost my breath.

My fall was stopped by a terrible splash, followed by total darkness! A minute later, my box began to rise until I was able to see light. I had fallen into the sea and was alive, thanks to what I imagine was an attack on the eagle by several others who had chased him to steal

The Box Tossed Up and Down.

his victim.

Now that I was gently bobbing about on top of the water, I slowly eased myself out of my hammock and used my sword to push open the small flap on the roof of the box to let in some air.

Then my thoughts wandered to my little nurse. "My poor Glumdalclitch! How she'll grieve for me! And she'll probably be blamed for losing me when it wasn't even her fault. She'll surely be banished from Court."

But for the next several hours, my concerns turned to my own welfare. Any moment now I feared that my box would be smashed to pieces against some rocks or overturned by a violent wave. "And even if I escape these dangers for a day or two," I told myself, "I'll surely die from hunger or from the cold out here alone at sea!"

On Top of the Water

"Do I Dare Hope?"

Chapter 15

An Amazing Rescue

As I sat bemoaning my fate, I heard, or thought I heard, a kind of scratching noise coming from one side of my box, the side that had no windows. It was the side where the two strong hooks had been used to fastened my box to a rider's belt.

Then I felt, or imagined I felt, the box being towed along in the sea. During this time, the waves rose to the top of my windows, leaving me almost in darkness, then dropped away, letting me see daylight again.

"Do I dare hope that someone is out there

rescuing me?" I wondered. "But how could it be possible?"

I immediately unscrewed one of my chairs from its place near the table, then screwed it back down on the floor directly below the flap I had opened on the roof. I climbed up on the chair and, with my mouth as close to the opening as possible, I shouted for help, over and over, in as many languages as I knew.

I then tied my handkerchief to the tip of my sword and pushed it through the hole. As I waved it frantically, I told myself, "Perhaps if a ship is near, the seamen will see that there's a poor soul inside this box even if they can't hear me call."

But all my shouting and waving were of no use. My box continued to be pulled along for the next hour until I felt it slam against something hard. Then I heard the noise of a chain being pulled through the ring on my roof, and I felt my box slowly being lifted out of the water.

I Shouted for Help.

I pushed my sword and handkerchief through the opening again and repeated my calls for help until I was hoarse.

Suddenly, feet began trampling on my roof, followed by voices—Englishmen's voices!—shouting to each other.

Then, through the opening in my roof, came the words, "If there's anyone inside this box, speak up now!"

"I'm here!" I called with a joy I never believed I could feel. "I'm an Englishman who's just gone through the worst disaster anyone ever experienced. I beg you, please rescue me from this box, from this prison I'm in."

"You'll be fine, my good man," replied the voice. "We've got you fastened to our ship, and we're sending our carpenter down to saw open the top of your box to let you out."

"You needn't do that," I shouted. "It'll take too much time. Just let one of your crew put his finger in the ring at the top and pull the entire box with me in it out of the sea."

Feet Tramping on the Roof

"Ha! He expects *one man* to pull a twelve-foot wooden box onto the ship with just his finger!" called a voice from above. "He must be mad!"

"What does he think we are—giants?" called another voice.

I later understood these reactions, for it never occurred to me that I was now among my own people, people of my own size and my own strength.

Within a few minutes, the carpenter was on top of the box and, in a while, had sawed a hole about four feet across. He let down a ladder for me to climb up, and I was taken aboard the ship, weak but overjoyed.

The crew were all amazed that I had been living in a box, "a mighty chest," they called my bedroom box, and they asked me a thousand questions about it.

I was in no condition to answer any of them just yet, and when the captain saw that I was ready to faint, he ordered his men to take me

He Let Down a Ladder for Me.

to his cabin. There, I was given some food and put to bed.

Before I went to sleep, I explained to the captain, "Sir, I have some very valuable furniture in my box—a bed, a cabinet, two chairs, a table, a hammock, and fine silk quilting on my walls. If you'll have one of your sailors bring them here, I'll show you proof of where I've been."

The captain agreed to have it done while I slept. I was glad, though, not to have seen the crew carry out his orders, for they tore the furniture from the floor, instead of unscrewing it, and ripped the quilting from the walls, badly damaging everything. Then they broke apart the box and stored the boards on the ship. Whatever remained when they were done, they let sink to the bottom of the sea.

I slept for hours, disturbed by dreams of Brobdingnag and the dangers I had escaped. When I awoke, it was about eight o'clock in the evening, and the captain invited me to have

I Was Given Food and Put to Bed.

dinner with him. During the meal, he was very kind and patient, and explained how he happened to find me.

"It was about noon today. I was looking through my telescope when I happened to spot that monstrous wooden chest you were in. I was too far away to make out exactly what it was, so I sent some men in my longboat to find out. Well, you can imagine how frightened they were when they came back to report that they had discovered a swimming house!

"I laughed at them, of course, but went back out with them to see what craziness they were talking about. I also took along a strong chain, just in case we wanted to take this strange object back to the ship."

"And I'm so pleased that you did, sir."

"Well, I saw the windows in your swimming house and the hooks on one side. I had my men fasten the chain to one of the hooks and we towed the house back to the ship. There, we fastened another chain onto the ring at the top

Dinner with the Captain

and raised it. But we could only get it three feet out of the water with our pulleys."

"And that's when I stuck my sword and handkerchief out of the hole at the top and called to you."

"Yes, and that's when I realized that some poor soul was inside."

"Tell me, captain, at about that time did you notice any large birds flying about?"

"Why, yes. We saw three eagles in the distance. They were very high up, so I couldn't tell their size, but they didn't seem any larger than eagles we usually see."

"And how far were we from land when you rescued me?"

"At least three hundred miles."

"That's impossible!" I exclaimed. "I had only been away from Brobdingnag two hours before I was dropped into the sea. I couldn't have traveled that far from land."

"Brobdingnag?" he said, looking at me strangely. "Are you sure you're feeling well,

"We Saw Three Eagles in the Distance."

after all? Perhaps you need to rest your brain some more, my good man."

"No, sir, really I'm quite well and as sane as I've ever been in my life."

"Well then," he said seriously, "are you well enough to tell me of your travels and how you came to be set adrift in that monstrous wooden chest? Have you committed a crime? I've heard of criminals being set adrift as punishment. If that's the case with you, I'd be forced to put you ashore at the first port we reach."

"Please, captain, be patient and hear my story. I'll tell you everything that happened to me from the time I left England to the moment you discovered me."

He sat patiently for several hours, showing genuine interest in me as I related the events of the past two years of my life. When I had finished, I offered him proof of all that I had said.

I unlocked my cabinet, which had been brought to his cabin, and began removing my

"I'd Be Forced to Put You Ashore."

belongings. As I held up each treasure, I explained what it was.

"Here's a comb I made for myself. The backing is a piece of the Queen's thumbnail I saved when she cut her nails, and the teeth are hairs from the King's beard when the royal barbers shaved him.

"And here's a gold ring the Queen gave me from her little finger. She put it over my head and around my neck like a collar.

"And look at these trousers. They were made for me by the royal tailor from the skin of a mouse.

"And see this tooth. The royal dentist pulled it from a footman's mouth."

On and on I went, showing the captain all my treasures. When I had finished, I asked him to please accept the gold ring as my thanks for rescuing me.

"No, Dr. Gulliver," he replied. "But what I would really enjoy having is that tooth from the footman's mouth. It's most amazing to see

A Gold Ring the Queen Gave Me

a tooth that measures a foot long and four inches across!"

I gladly made him a present of the tooth.

The rest of the voyage back to England took about nine months. During that time, we stopped at many ports for food and water, but I never went ashore with the longboat. I never went ashore again until we were back on English soil!

As the captain and I parted, he made a strange request. "Dr. Gulliver, I hope one day you'll write a book about your travels. I'm sure the world would be interested in reading about your adventures."

"I really think the world has quite enough travel books, and really, who would believe all that has happened to me? After all, I can't present my proof to the world, as I've presented it to you."

I found that even my wife and family had difficulty believing what I told them. That may be why they insisted that I never go to sea

My Family Had Difficulty Believing Me.

again.

Still, my destiny was not to stay on land for long. My destiny was to make many more voyages.

And that, my young readers, is another story...

13820

Made in the USA
Monee, IL
26 February 2021